Level 1
Ready to Catch Reader

How to Catch
stories!

From the
New York Times bestselling team
**Adam Wallace
& Andy Elkerton**

sourcebooks
wonderland

First published in 2021 by Sourcebooks Wonderland.
Collective Goods special edition published in 2022.
P.O. Box 4410, Naperville, Illinois 60567-4410
(630) 961-3900
sourcebookskids.com

Source of Production: Wing King Tong Paper Products Co. Ltd.,
Shenzhen, Guangdong Province, China
Date of Production: July 2022
Run Number: 5027662

Printed and bound in China.
WKT 10 9 8 7 6 5 4 3 2 1

Learning to read is as easy as 1, 2, 3!

DEAR GROWN-UP:

Are you ready to catch unicorns, dinosaurs, mermaids, and more? From the *New York Times* bestselling brand that both kids and parents love, we proudly present: Ready to Catch Reader!

Our goal—help kids get caught reading and become independent readers! **READY TO CATCH** will improve reading skills while immersing children into the wonderful world of How to Catch.

So have your special Catch Club Kid grab their net and a comfy chair and get ready to go on a reading adventure!

Level 1: Beginner Reader
Pre K–Grade 1
Easy vocabulary. Short sentences. Word repetition. Simple content and stories. Correlation between art and text.

Level 2: Emerging Reader
Kindergarten–Grade 2
Letter blends. Compound sentences. Contractions. Simple, high-interest storylines. Art offers visual cues to decipher text.

Level 3: Reading Alone
Grade 1–Grade 3
Longer, more complex storylines. Story told in paragraph form. Character development. More challenging letter blends and multisyllable words. Art enhances the story.

Level 1 Ready to Catch Reader

Contents

How to Catch a Dinosaur

Adam Wallace & Andy Elkerton

Tomorrow is the
big science fair.
Each year I try to win.
But I have not won yet.

This year I know I will win.

I have a plan.

This year I am going to catch a dinosaur.

Crocodiles and sharks lived
when the dinosaurs ruled.
They are still here.

That means dinosaurs must
still be here too!
We just need to find one.

First, we go to the park.
We need to find
the dinosaur's trail.
What is that thing over there?

Could it be?

Yes!

It is a dinosaur tail.

KEEP OFF
GRASS

We learned in class that
dinosaurs were not like
crocodiles.

They were more like birds.

Look what the dinosaur left behind.

It is our first clue!

Uh-oh.

The dinosaur skipped right past our volcano.

She did not even look!

She did like the Venus flytrap.

She munched it right in two.

I guess this dinosaur is

a plant eater!

That dinosaur is as
fast as the wind.
She ran right by our trap.

It is a good thing

we have more traps planned.

This dinosaur is onto

all my tricks!

She knows how each trap works.

I wonder if she was watching when I tested them.

Oh no!

She slipped right past us!

And that is not all.

She ruined Mom's best roses!

Maybe the dinosaur
just needs a friend.

She will not be able to resist
the playground we made.

Oh no.

We missed again!

Our trap had pulleys.

It had ropes and decks.

But the dinosaur did not care!

She smashed it to bits.

She should be called T. Wrecks.

This dinosaur is slippery.
But we are not done yet.
My mom knows how
to build robots.

She has taught me
a trick or three.
The Robo-Hugger 3000
is sure to catch our girl.

Oh no.

That clever dinosaur

tricked our robot

by dressing like a bird.

If we do not catch that
dinosaur soon,
I will never win a prize!

We did not catch the dinosaur.

I do not know what to do.

Then my friends remind me...

We do have something to enter in the science fair!

Better luck next time!

How to Catch a Mermaid

Adam Wallace & Andy Elkerton

Last week I saw a mermaid.

I really did!

I want to catch her.

Then she can be my friend.

She could teach me about
mermaids.
She could show me her city.
We could swim all over!

I cannot catch her alone.

It will take a team.

You two come with me.

We need a plan!

First, we need to
build a trap.
Let us make one near
the tide pool!

Look at this box I found.
It is so shiny.
Mermaids love
shiny things.

She will not be able

to stay away.

Oh no.

It is in the water!

Look at this crown I found.

It is shiny too.

The mermaid will have to

come check it out.

My net is ready.
When she comes to
get the crown,
I will catch her!

Oh no.

She used some seaweed

to take the crown!

I need another plan.

I know!
I will put this
shiny necklace
inside a clam.

Oh no!

She put a rock

where the necklace was

to keep the clam from closing.

Now she has my necklace!
I need to come up with
a better trap!

I learned a trick
from the mermaid.
Look at my lasso.
I hid it in the seaweed.

Oh no.

She is too fast!

When will I catch

this tricky mermaid?

Maybe some music will
draw her in!
Let us try some funky beats.

Uh-oh.

The sharks like

our music too.

That was a close one!

The sharks almost got us!

It is a good thing we found
this cool submarine!

The sub has cool robot arms.
Maybe it can help us
catch our mermaid.

Oh no.

She got away again.

She is too fast!

It is time to
pull out all the stops.
Maybe this chest of gold
will win her over.

Oh no!

She is onto our trap.

The chest made
too much noise!

Uh-oh.

The sharks are back!

What are we going to do?

We used all our traps.

We are out of bait.

We need help.

But from who?

Look!

It is our mermaid.

She made a trap

to save us!

She scares the sharks
and scoops us up.
She is really brave.

Thanks to our mermaid,
we are safely
back on land.

We will miss her
and her tricky ways.
We wish she could have stayed.

How to Catch a Dragon

Adam Wallace & Andy Elkerton

Mom is cooking
for the New Year.
Grandma is helping.

Mom says we need a dragon.

They are good luck.

Dragons bring health and money.

My friends and I
always hang red lanterns
for the New Year.

This year we have a new job.

We are looking for a dragon.

Look over there!

A real dragon's tail!

To catch a dragon
we need a trap.
I know!
We will make a slide.

Uh-oh.

This dragon is too smart.

And he can control the water!

This is not going to be easy.

I know!
We will make a web
out of noodles and
sticky rice!

That dragon really
liked our trap.
He liked it so much,
he ate it all up!

Those noodles should have made him sleepy.

But he went right past
our Dragon Inn!

We thought we could
lure him in
with a great beat.

But that dragon is a
better drummer
than I am!

Now we will
get him for sure.
Dragons love gold.

He will never be able
to say no
to this bait!

Oh no.

There is money falling

from the sky.

That is not good.
It means the dragon
got away again.

This last trap has to work.

It is our best chance.

If there is one thing dragons love,
it is the Dragon Dance.

Our Dragon Dance is
going great.

This is so much fun.

But where is our dragon?

Oh no.

What a mess!

And the dragon

got away again!

I am all out of ideas.
I guess that means
no health or money
this year.

"I am sorry, Mom,"
I say.
"I tried my best
to make you proud."

Mom gives me a big hug.

"It is okay," she says.

"I love this dragon
best of all."

Fireworks light up
the night sky.
Mom and I watch.
Grandma watches too.

Now I know.

I am already lucky.

I have the best family.

I do not need a dragon.

烟花

家庭

But that does not mean
I do not want one.

Better luck next year!

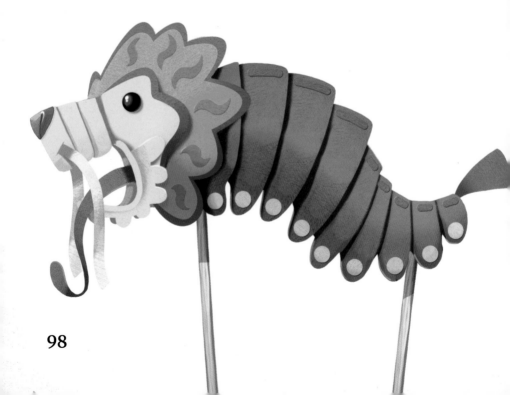

How to Catch
a Snowman

Adam Wallace & Andy Elkerton

The moon is full.

There is snow on the ground.

The time is right
for magic.

A magic star
shines down on me.
It brings me to life!

I do not want to play.

I do not give warm hugs.

I do not want anyone

to catch me.

But these kids will try.

They always do.

The first trap is
a good try.
It makes me smile.

But a web of scarfs
will not catch me.
Now you are the ones
left in a pile.

This next trap is better.

I almost do not

get away.

But I am sneaky.

I skate fast.

I spin.

Now you are the ones
covered in snow!

A snowman who loves summer?
I have never heard
of that before.

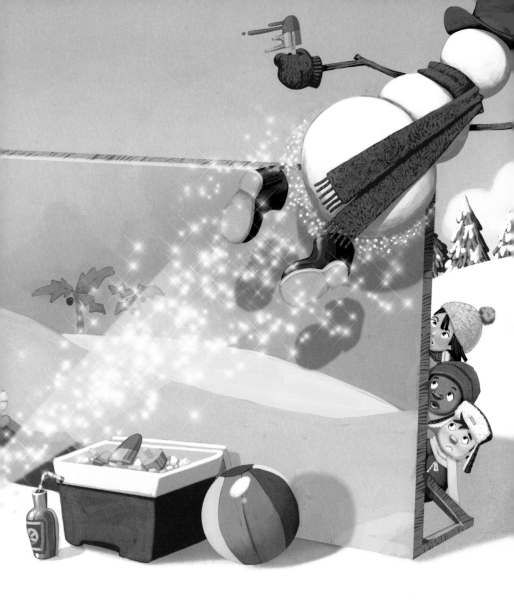

I bet you did not know
that I can fly.
Watch out.
Here I go!

Oh no.

This one almost got me.

You chased me right down that hill.

But I escaped again.

I turned into a big snowball

and rolled right away!

That next trick was

a good use of snow.

But you did not fool me.

Now look at this.

That is something new.

Your snow globe is nice.

But it will not hold me!

A snowman shop.

Now, that is a treat!

Maybe I will grab

a hat or some new gloves.

My nose is made
from a carrot.

But do you really think you can
catch me with one?

Now this is fun!

I love sledding down a slide.

But I think I will skip the
bounce at the end.

That trap was smart.

Good job!

But your water still
will not stop me!

I escaped your last trap.

It was a good game.

But now the sun is setting.

It is time to go inside.

You did not catch me.

That makes me the winner!

But maybe I can leave
a small gift for you.

I will see you next year!

Congratulations

127

How to Catch
a Unicorn

Adam Wallace & Andy Elkerton

It is a bright and shiny day.

I want something

fun to do!

I know!
I will ride a rainbow
right to the zoo!

Uh-oh.

The kids saw me.

If they catch me,
I will lose my magic!

My animal friends will not let me down.

With their help,

I know I can escape.

I stop to see the zebras.

Then I have to go.

KICK!

Do these kids really think

I will stop for a cool drink?

Unicorn
Lemonade

Next, they try to stop me
with a parachute.

But I am not that easy to catch!
All they find is a trail of glitter.

I chill with the penguins.

But I do not stay long.

This place is full of traps!

I need a better place
to hide out.

This room is so dark!
It is a good thing
I have my horn.

Who knows what I
might walk into
without its light.

Maybe I will go see
the butterflies.

The only way to fit in here
is to shrink my size!

My nose smells something sweet.

My little friends help out

while I take a bite.

Then I am off again!

Next, I go somewhere hot.

These kids think they can get me.

But the snakes and lizards
are ready to help!

Time to get big again!

I love these little monkeys,
but it is the giraffe
who saves the day!

What is that in the water?

That boat looks like fun.

I would stay in the water,
but my friends say I have to run.

My beaver friends show me
the kids' latest trap.

With one big bite,

they get rid of it for me.

The gift shop is a great place
to set their next trap.

It is a good thing there are
lots of things to take my place.

I had fun today.

The zoo has been a blast.

You tried your best,

but unicorns are hard to catch.

Keep up the good work.

Keep trying all those traps.

I will be back again.

Maybe next time you will get me!

Better luck next time!

How to Catch
a Monster

Adam Wallace & Andy Elkerton

My school is having a play.

We each have a part.

I get to be the

Ninja Master!

I feel brave and strong.

I feel like a hero!

Now, there is just
one thing to do.

There is a monster
in my closest.
He has big claws
and sharp teeth.

At night he comes
to scare me.
But tonight
I will catch him!

I see my monster right away.

He is trying out his roar.

He wants to scare me.

But I am a hero now.

I will not be scared.

Not by a monster.

To catch my monster

I will need some good traps.

It is a good thing I have
a trick or two up my sleeve.

Uh-oh.

This monster is stronger
than I thought.

That is okay.

I am not done yet.

I will get him with my

Ninja-Nabbing Net!

Oh no.

He escaped again.

This next trap is
sure to get him!

I got him this time.
Now he cannot scare me
anymore.

I look at the monster.

He seems sad.

"I am sorry," I say.

"But no more scaring."

"I did not mean to scare you,"
the monster says.
"I just wanted to
play with you."

"It is hard to play
when you are asleep.
That is why I
tried to wake you."

I stop my ninja bot.

The monster pulls the bars apart.

He smiles.

Then he farts!

The fart smells like

strawberries and lime.

"That is how monsters
say hello!" he says.

The monster takes me
to his house.

I meet his mom and dad.

He is not so scary after all!

We play for hours.

He throws me in the air
and we eat volcano pie.

When it is time for bed,
he helps me brush my teeth.

He squeezes out all my toothpaste.
Boy, is he strong!

Mom tucks me in.

She turns off the light.

But I do not worry.

I am home, safe and sound.

I know what is in the closet.

It is my monster!

Now he does not scare me.

He is my friend!